## Amazon Reviews for St(

I find that many books merge i mind and after a year or so I can't remember what it was about, or even what I found so special about it. With Steve Roach you know you'll never read another story like his. His work has a way of fixing itself in your mind forever. These stories are often not a comfortable read but if you want your ideas stretched and challenged, have a go.
**Ignite, Amazon Review and Vine Voice.**

This is a gem floating among the flotsam of self published stories on Amazon. The author grabs the attention of the reader early with a dark yarn told over a cold brew in worn down pub by the sea. What better place to hear a frightening tale of the black depths? Overtones of Poe can be felt throughout and the story didn't falter once as the horror continued to build.
**Amazon.com review of The Whaler**

I found the historical period to be accurately depicted, the gloomy coastal and shipboard settings to all ring true, and the central characters to have some genuine depth. With convincing scenery put quickly and efficiently in place and competent actors on the stage, the author proceeded to roll out a period American horror tale that kept me awake later than I had originally intended. I found myself needing to read just one more page until the entire story was satisfyingly done. That, in my opinion, is the sign of a well-made tale.
**Amazon.com review of The Whaler**

*It's a well told tale and the descriptions of the hardships of life aboard a whaling ship, especially during the butchering, flensing and rendering stages are graphic and believable. I live near a town with a museum largely dedicated to the old whaling fleets and I've seen some of the tools used. Steve Roach knows of what he speaks.*
**Amazon UK review of The Whaler**

*I quite enjoyed this short story and despite it's bleak content felt it was well written and thought provoking. The blurb hinted at the dark turn the story takes yet I was still shocked by the finale. I felt there were various layers of hidden narratives; the cruelty of children, loyalty of a beloved pet and almost a Karmic climax.*
**Amazon UK review of A Dog's Life**

*I enjoyed this, it was a nice little read on a warm evening and I can honestly say I loved it, well written, poignant and engrossing, I just wish it had been longer, if I hadn't read it one sitting it would have been one of those books I would have laid awake at night thinking about and read some more as soon as I woke up next morning.*
**Amazon UK review of A Dog's Life**

*This is, without a doubt, the darkest and most disturbing book I've ever read....and I've read many. I will spend the rest of my life trying to forget it and wishing I'd never purchased it. I worry about the author.*
**Amazon.com review of A Dog's Life**

*The growing relationship between the man and the spider is a delight as we watch it unfold. Steve Roach has a dark side to his humour though. Things go downhill! This is a short story but as there's a small cast there is time for character development and the plot has a slight inevitability although I didn't see the final page coming. The author's writing style is skilful and accessible without being in any way simple. Short but sweet, this one, and well worth a read.*
**Amazon UK review of The Farda**

*Describing the ugliness that can happen in life is a delicate business, something that is handled sensitively in this unusual tale. It draws you in in a menacing way, and within its obvious desire to shock it also carefully balances a very human story throughout. Raw and thought provoking, I found it to be well written and an enjoyable read, which surprised me given the nature of its subject matter.*
**Amazon UK review for Bébé**

*This is a dark tale about a child born from a sexual assault that handles the subject in an honest manner. As a previous reviewer quite rightly said it is raw and thought provoking in a way that is both careful & sensitive. That being said, this book is not really for the faint-hearted or sensitive reader.*
**Amazon UK review for Bébé**

*This can't be called an enjoyable book; it's horrifying and fascinating though. Steve Roach often pushes at the boundaries of destructive relationships. It makes for the sort of book from which you can't look away - like a road accident. As I said, it's wrong to say it's enjoyable,*

*showing as it does, scenes of abuse. It's a hard book to put down though!*
**Amazon UK review for Bébé**

*This, although ostensibly a story about fraternal hatred (it's much more than simple sibling rivalry!) seems rather deeper than its surface story. Twins who fought even in the womb and who spent their childhood fighting to the extent they were regulars at A&E finally seem to settle to ignoring one another. However, a love feud results directly in the death of one and indirectly the death of the other. We have all heard the term, 'Death is not the end,' and that's so true here. The depth of their mutual hatred is such that they still try to find ways to annihilate each other. The story, through some interesting descriptive prose, takes us much further, deeper, than you would imagine. Can hatred ever die? They say love never dies and hatred is just the other side of the coin. This is another intriguing idea from a man who can really come up with a good story line. The writing style is clear and unfussy but Steve Roach can use language well and pull the reader into a darned good tale.*
**Amazon UK review for Twins**

*Another corker from Steve Roach. Amazing, thought provoking, scary stuff. Timeless – tackles our basic human insecurities.*
**Amazon UK Review for All That Will Be Lost**

# The Whaler

© Steve Roach 2024
Originally published 2011.

The right of Steve Roach to be identified
as the author of this work has been asserted
in accordance with Section 77 of the
Copyright, Designs and Patents Act 1988.

No part of this book may be reproduced or distributed in any form or by any means, electronic or mechanical, or stored in a database or retrieval system, without prior written consent from
the author.

Cover design by Lloyd Hollingworth.

Thanks to Steph Smith, Lloyd Hollingworth and anybody who has supported me over the years.

**Facebook.com/writerroach**

# The Whaler

# The Whaler

## One

I had no business in America. I had come to make my fortune and had failed, miserably. They said there was gold in the hills out West, but I found nothing other than dead things and lawlessness. I gave away my prospecting equipment and gave up on the dream of a new life, heading back to the eastern seaboard on foot, relying upon the kindness of strangers to survive.

I was in New Bedford to try and make my way back home to England, tail between my legs, humbled.

New Bedford was an old town, for this part of the world. The houses lining the streets leading to the harbour were run down, worn out and crumbling from perhaps two full centuries of aging in the salty air hereabouts. The coloured paints they used were faded and flaking. Even the people I saw appeared decrepit and stooped, older than their years.

If I could find passage on a ship I was prepared to work hard and pay my way with labour. My immediate plan was to put the word out with the locals and wait. Somebody, somewhere, would sail for Europe, I was certain of it. If there was a delay in procuring passage, I would look for work until a ship was ready.

As I neared the harbour, the sounds of industry grew louder. There were more people here, not all of them friendly. A beggar shouted something at me, remonstrating with me for ignoring him and not providing him with money. In all seriousness, he was probably better off than I was – perhaps I should have been the one asking him for a handout. I had little more than a few coins in my pockets, and if I didn't find a place on a ship I would probably end up on the streets, a daunting prospect at the best of times, but with a harsh, imminent New England winter it was a prospect that would more than likely see me dead in a gutter within days, frozen solid and covered with a blanket of thick snow.

I was approached by a prostitute touting for business. It had been a long time since I had intimately known another person, and just the thought of touching her skin brought on a sadness that felt like a dead weight inside, a realisation of just how lonely I was. If I'd had money to spare, I would have succumbed to her dubious charms, but I was forced to merely smile, and carry on.

I reached the harbour, and looked out upon the sea. Thousands of miles across that heaving body of water lay my home soil. It may just as well have been on the moon. A number of ships were anchored a short distance out, rolling with the restless waves. The incoming tide smashed repeatedly into the harbour wall, sending up great plumes of spray that settled on a group of low buildings, one of which was a tavern. It had been this way for centuries, and my passing through this place would leave no mark. Long after I had gone, things would be exactly the same.

I entered the tavern and waited for my eyes to adjust to the gloom. It was mostly empty, save for one or two old gents nursing their beers, hunched little men in a room full of stale air and old smoke. They stared at me, openly. One of them was missing an eye, having a dark and empty socket on one side of his face. I nodded and turned away before my own staring became an obvious rudeness. I walked over to the bar, where I ordered a beer from the barman.

'Would you know of any boats heading for Europe?' I asked him.

'No boats going to Europe,' he said, with something of an unfriendly sneer. 'Ships maybe. No boats.'

So I'd found myself an idiot. There are plenty of them in this world, sure enough, and they are all equally tiresome. What kind of a man takes pleasure belittling a stranger simply because of incorrect nautical terminology? Is it really worth the effort? I paid him and grabbed my drink without thanks, and sat on a bench near to the window. Great clouds of spray threw themselves over the harbour wall and settled on the window, making everything blurry outside.

'Heading for Europe, then?' asked a voice.

I turned to see one of the old men staring at me. It was him with the missing eye.

'What of it?' I asked.

'I know of a ship bound for Marseilles in three days. Would that do you?'

'It's a start,' I said. 'I'm heading for England, if there's anything bound that way.'

He shook his head slowly, and smiled a grin made of perhaps three teeth. 'You won't get anything bound for England,' he said. 'There's nothing there worth the journey.'

I had to smile at his directness. It appeared that men were rude around these parts, at least the ones I had met so far, but at least this old fool had a sense of humour about him. Marseilles. It would still be something of a stretch to get back home on my limited funds but I would be on the right continent. Maybe I had been lucky by even finding a ship bound for Europe.

'Then Marseilles will do me,' I said. 'Who do I speak to?'

'My son,' he said. 'He'll be here shortly. Come, sit with me.'

I picked up my beer and joined the old man at his table. It was hard to tell his age, though it was certainly great. His face was as weathered as the facades of the crumbling cottages I'd passed on my way to the harbour. His one eye looked like a black jewel, shining with a fierce intelligence. The other was an empty socket, the eyelid raised and providing no cover for the red, moist hole in his face. It was hard not to stare. His chin sported a thick, shaggy beard, and his hair had been cut short with a severity that left only grey stubble behind.

'You're from the old country, then,' he said.

'England, you mean?'

'Aye. Most of us hereabouts have ancestry buried in England, but not one of us still living would swap for this. You're in God's country now, lad.'

'Is that so?' I asked him, smiling. 'When you have finished pouring scorn on my homeland, would you care for another beer whilst we wait for your son?'

'I would,' he said, tipping the dregs of his ale down his bearded throat. I glanced over at the bartender.

'Another one here,' I said. Whilst we waited for the old man's drink to be brought over, we sat regarding each other in silence for a few moments. His was easy company. Despite his lively tongue, I found myself liking him.

'You want to know about the eye?' he said at last.

I feigned disinterest but he had me. Of course I wanted to know about the eye. Any man who sees another missing an eye is naturally curious, and the more he protests disinterest the greater the liar. The barman set the drink down on the table, disturbing us, and stood hovering. I started searching my pockets for change and the old man looked up at the barman and told him to add the charge to his tab.

'I'm supposed to be buying you a drink,' I said. He waved a hand in a dismissive gesture.

'It doesn't matter, really,' he said, smiling. 'Now then, what do you know of whaling, lad?'

'Whaling? Nothing at all.'

TWO

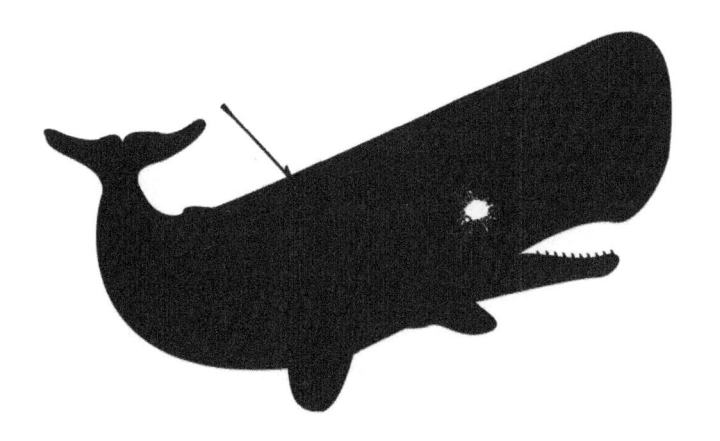

## Two

'You are in the whaling capital of the world,' he said, gesturing at the blurry scenery just outside the window. 'Men from these parts have plied the trade for centuries, and for a long time I was one of them. In the old days, before my time, the carcasses used to wash up on the beach and the Indians would strip them down. By the time I started, it wasn't just the Indians that needed what the whale could give – the whole world was gripped by whale-fever.

'Never was a more useful creature invented by God! Without whale oil, man would live in darkness. There would be no perfume to keep the dainty lady-folk from stinking. Machinery would seize up, and industry would come to a grinding halt. Can you imagine that?'

'I haven't really given it much thought.'

'The disappearance of the whale would cause the very world to end! Ever seen a whale?'

'Once, when I first landed in New York. I saw a group of them.'

'A pod, you mean. Beautiful creatures, aren't they? I've helped to kill hundreds in my time. I did my bit to hold the darkness back and keep machines lubricated, for what it's worth.'

He smiled sadly, and took a sip of his ale. Then, with a little grunt of discomfort, he bent down to his overcoat on the stool next to him, reached into the pocket and pulled out a pipe and a small tin of tobacco. I watched as he went about his pipe-work, a routine that he had obviously perfected over the years. He tapped the head onto the table and inspected it before taking out a pinch of tobacco and pressing it down. He lit a match and sucked at the pipe until the tobacco was lit, and thick curls of blue smoke rose up towards the dirty ceiling.

'I hunted whales,' he said grimly, 'until the waters of New England were virtually empty. Each time we went to sea, we went that little bit further to find them, until we eventually pitched up on the other side of the world. In the end, we were away for two years at a time. How long was your voyage to New York, lad?'

'Five weeks.'

'That's hardly enough time to get the ship wet! It might have felt like a long time but believe me, when you're at sea for two years it'll leave a mark on your very soul. You forget what land feels like, and maybe even forget what it looks like. The entire world is in constant motion, shifting and rolling, up and down, heave and ho! And yet, there are places where the very same oceans are stagnant and still, with nary a sniff of a breeze! I've seen many strange things, in my time, and most of them involve the sea. What about you?'

'What about me?'

'Tell me about the strangest thing you ever saw.'

'Well, your eye is pretty strange.'

He hooted with laughter and slapped the table in a show of good humour. This eruption quickly descended into a coughing fit, and for a moment I thought he was choking to death. I stood, about to do something – anything – but he held up a hand to ward me off and, with a rattle of strenuous hacking, coughed up a thick gob of phlegm and spat it onto the floor. The barman looked over with evident disgust but said nothing.

'Anything else?' asked the old man, now sufficiently recovered to continue.

'I've seen a tornado – does that count?'

'Aye, that counts. I've seen one myself, out on the South Atlantic – a great twisting column of briny water that stretched up into the sky! But it's not the weirdest thing I ever saw. That would be the whale. Yes, I have no doubts about it. We found one with something rotten inside it - rotten and black and alive!'

'What was it?'

'Ha! If only I knew! I was a whaler for the better part of fifty years. Made it all the way to First Mate, and should've had my own ship but I was too fond of the drink and I didn't want the responsibility that comes with the position of Captain. First Mate was good enough for me. Easy enough, if you know what you're doing, little more than keeping log and inventory, and noting down all that things that happen on board. Each whale we caught, it was my job to note down the haul once we'd stripped it down. So, I was a pencil-pusher.

'The men liked me well enough, I think. They're a rough breed, whalers. Some of them would murder you if you looked at them the wrong way. I once saw a whaler gut one of his friends over a derogatory comment involving his mother. Yes, they're very rough characters. And all of them, to the last one, were terrified of the Captain.

'It's common knowledge that the Captains of whaling ships are a breed of men more deranged than most, but Grice was the worst these parts have ever known. Nobody liked him, not even his wife. And he hated everybody right back. He was a stone-hearted bastard, full of hate for the world and everything in it, but he had a special kind of hate for whales. He exulted in their murder. The only time I ever saw him crack a smile was when he was knee deep in whale blood.

'Killing was the only thing that gave him pleasure, and the bigger the thing he could kill, the happier he was. If whales didn't exist, he would have been out on the plains of Africa, bringing down elephants. Or maybe hunting men through the streets of New England. He was that kind of man. Dangerous. Unhinged.'

He trailed off for a moment and took a sip of his beer. We were surrounded by a fug of fresh tobacco smoke, giving the musty air inside tavern a slightly blue tinge, and though I had no time for engaging in the dirty habit myself, I found the aroma pleasant enough.

'Now then,' continued the old man. 'The Nautilus left New Bedford in December '52, and we sailed East, cutting down through the North and South Atlantic and rounding the Horn in a storm that almost wrecked us. After months at sea, we reached our hunting grounds in the South Pacific.

'Now you say you've seen a pod of whales off the coast of New York, and it's likely you'd have seen sperm whales. They are enormous, magnificent creatures. I've seen them more than 60 feet long, and they can weigh 40 tons. Bear in mind that the Nautilus herself was only 87 feet, so we were hunting beasts that were almost the size of the ship. A single whale can yield more than 20 barrels of oil, and by the time we found the whale that did for Captain Grice, we must have had more than 200 filled barrels in the hold, and 6 tons of baleen we'd stripped from smaller whales we found on our route.

'This whale was alone. The lookout spotted it and we dropped the boats into the water. Grice took captaincy of the first. Normally, the Captain would stay aboard the ship and let his men go about the business of killing the whale, but not Grice. I took charge of the middle boat and the Second Mate took charge of the third. We fanned out and approached the whale from behind.

'I could see there was something wrong with it immediately. It moved in a very odd manner. It kept coughing through its blowhole, sick and probably dying already. We were almost upon it before the whale suspected we were there, and the harpooners were readying themselves to throw. We had three of them, one in each boat, and they were all Indians - two Narrangansets and a Wampanoag. They were fearless and no white man could match them for skill with a harpoon.

'Grice couldn't contain himself. "KILL IT!" he screamed, and the Indian in his boat launched a harpoon and it struck home. The whale thrashed and set off at a rate of knots, dragging the boat behind it. A strong adult whale can pull a boat for two hours, bouncing and crashing on the waves in its wake. It's called the Nantucket Sleigh Ride for good reason. It wasn't uncommon for men to be thrown clear in the turmoil. Once, a whale managed to get all of us thrown out and it disappeared with the empty boat, and we never saw it again.

'The kills were rarely easy, even with old or sick whales. In the hundreds of encounters I was directly involved with, there was always something that happened that wasn't supposed to. Sometimes, a whale can turn, and it ducks under the boat and rises up out of the water with enough force to smash it to kindling. If that happens, the whale often likes to come back for the men, and I've seen quite a few killed this way. Thomas Essex was taken in the jaws of one and sunk to the bottom of the ocean, straight to meet with Davy Jones. I remember I had to tell his wife, and she lost her unborn with the shock of it.

'But this one was extremely weak, and happened to be one of those whales that gave us nothing in the way of trouble. After no more than a few minutes it gave up the chase, exhausted. As the trailing boats caught up, Grice grabbed a lance and stabbed it, and a terrible shriek came out of its blowhole. It's a ghastly sound. I heard it many times, over the years, and never did get used to it.

'They have a language to themselves, these creatures – snorts and barks, moans and howls and clicks and coughs – you wouldn't credit a whale with enough intelligence to make their feelings known through sounds, but you'd be wrong, lad.

'When you kill one, you have to aim for the lungs – the heart is too deep and the brain is protected by the skull. Skilled folk can do it with a single blow, but Grice preferred to stab aimlessly, over and over, plunging the lance into the whale with the intention of making it suffer before it died. The sea was turning red and that whale was coughing and throwing up a fountain of blood through its blowhole, vomiting a curtain of half-digested squid and other muck.

Grice kept an axe in his boat for moments such as this. He grabbed it and jumped out onto the whale, striding out until he found a secure position and then he started to swing.

'Now, there's no rhyme or reason for a man to attack a whale with an axe. The beast was dying from lance-wounds, and an axe would make no real difference to its demise. It would only cause it further pain. The men in his boat sat down and watched, and when we drew level we did the same thing. We knew that this was the way Grice was, and there was no arguing with him, no reasoning. He lifted the axe and brought it down into the whale, over and over, gathering speed as the frenzy of violence overcame him completely. His eyes were glazed and he was in his special place, and as the whale rolled Grice kept his footing and started to attack the exposed belly.

'We had to wait until he tired himself out. When he finally climbed back down into the boat, nobody spoke. He dropped the axe with a clatter and sat staring out to sea, as if awakening from a dream. The whale was a mess, its blubber all gouged and hacked, and the men were none too pleased because it makes the flensing an even more difficult job. But nobody remonstrated with him – it was his ship, after all, and it was as plain as day that Grice wasn't right in the head. Anybody who confronted him was likely to end up in the same state as the whale.

'So the other boats hooked up their harpoon lines and we rowed the corpse back to the Nautilus. Sometimes, when we'd killed a strong, healthy whale, it would drag us miles from the ship, and it would be dark by the time we reached her, but this whale didn't make it so far and we had daylight left to get started. We got the mast-hook into the carcass and lifted it up to starboard, and began stripping the blubber.

'We worked through the night and into the next day. That was how it was with whales, you spent days, sometimes weeks looking for them and doing little else besides, but when you found one it was all hands on deck. Strips of blubber were brought onto the ship and chopped into smaller pieces for rendering. This coated the deck in blood and strings of fat, and it would mark the start of a few days where keeping your footing was all but impossible.

'The trywork burners were started up and the blubber was boiled down. It's a business that's almost as grisly as the killing itself. As the blubber starts to render, it gives off a vile, thick smoke, and there's no escaping it. Black and greasy, it settles onto the masts and marks the sails. It stains your clothes and forces its way into your lungs, a stinking, choking mass that settles over the ship for days, hovering like a cloud of doom.

'When that job was finally completed, we cut off the head and brought it on deck, and one of the men drilled into the spermaceti reservoir. This is the mother lode when it comes to whaling – the purest of the oils and the most valuable. It doesn't need processing; it's simply scooped out and poured into barrels. We got twenty barrels of spermaceti out of that whale, and after so long at sea the hold was almost full. We were one catch away from coming home.

'Sharks were circling, waiting for us to let the rest of the carcass fall back into the water. There must have been a hundred of them, thrashing and roiling next to the ship, so densely packed together that it was almost like a single, snarling entity continually turning itself inside out, a writhing beast that stared up at the ship with hundreds of bulging, black eyes, anticipating the meal to come. It's a terrifying sight, but one so common amongst whalers that many simply ignore it altogether, but I never could. Grice would often have a go at harpooning one or two sharks himself, just for the hell of it. There was so many it was impossible to miss. A harpooned shark would be turned on by the others, and as they all began to bite each other, the waters would erupt in a frenzy of blood and gnashing teeth, and Grice would stand and laugh as they tore each other to pieces. Even though I hated what Grice had done, I always watched this bloody spectacle – however hard I tried I just couldn't tear my gaze away from the carnage.

'As he stood on the cutting platform, he called for one of the Indians to pass him a harpoon but then something caught his eye and he lowered himself down onto the carcass. It was slippery and stank to high Heaven, and a highly dangerous undertaking when there were hungry sharks waiting, should you miss your footing. He got down on his knees and poked around amongst the ribs. After a few minutes, he called for the Indians to bring the cutting spades and they set to work on the carcass, chopping out something that the rest of us couldn't see. Grice kept shouting at the Indians, forcing them to keep at it. It was as though they were afraid, but they were more afraid of Grice and kept working.

'Eventually, the mast-hook brought it up onto the deck. We all stood around, looking at it. It was the queerest thing I'd ever seen, a black gelatinous mass about the size of a man, and it seemed to have one large, milky eye that moved and looked at each of us in turn. We could see a black pupil enlarging and contracting as it focussed. Whatever this thing was, it appeared to be alive. When it caught my eye, I felt a shiver of horror and revulsion pass right through me.'

As the old man recounted this part of his story, I saw his posture stiffen at the memory. He shook himself down and blew air through his lips. I took this as a natural break to signal the barman and order more drinks – mine was empty and with a few quick swigs he downed the remains of his. Whilst we waited, he tapped out his pipe and put a fresh batch of tobacco into it. The barman brought over two more beers and walked away.

'Hey,' I called after him. He stopped and turned. 'We appear to be the only people keeping you in business. How about you show some appreciation for that?'

He rolled his eyes and walked off, disappearing through a doorway behind the bar.

"Miserable bastard," I muttered.

The old man smiled, and puffed at his pipe until it shrouded us once more in the sweet smell of burnt tobacco.

'So what was this thing you found?' I asked.

'We thought perhaps a tumour of some sort. Grice ordered it to be taken down into the hold and had one of the men keep watch over it. The Indians had conferred between themselves and stood apart from the rest of the crew, wanting nothing to do with this thing. I think they believed it was the reincarnation of some dark spirit, or some other such nonsense. They have some strange beliefs, Indians.

'Anyway, to all intents and purposes that marked the end of the voyage. Within two days, Grice made the order that we sail home, and for the next two months that's what we did. We caught two more baleens on the way, but Grice's heart wasn't in it. He spent a considerable amount of time below deck, studying this thing we'd found, and eventually had it moved to his cabin. By the time we landed, we hadn't seen him for days, and he left the ship immediately, taking the thing with him in a damned wheelbarrow, covered in one of the spare sails. I was left in charge of unloading the ship, selling off the various oils and baleen, and ensuring the men were paid.

'So began our shore leave. Usually, we whalers get restless after a few weeks, and begin gearing up for a new expedition relatively quickly. You'd think that was strange, and it is, but that's how it is. At sea, with little to do and no human contact apart from the men you share the ship with, you get the homesickness, and then within a few weeks of returning to Civilisation you get the urge to shun it once more, to head back out to sea and let everything else go to hell. It's a paradox we learn to live with.

'After two months, I still hadn't heard anything from Grice, so I went to his house. His wife Bess answered the door and she looked terrible, as though she'd aged twenty years since last I saw her. She told me Grice was unwell, and made me stand on the front step whilst she went back inside and spoke with him. He wasn't up to seeing me, but he gave the order to make preparations for a new voyage, to sail on the first of the following month.

'So that's what I did. I rounded up the crew and we prepared the Nautilus.

# THREE

## Three

'On the morning of the first, we waited. The sun wasn't yet up. Everybody was aboard except Grice and we were starting to get impatient, itching to leave. It was highly unusual for him to be so late. There came a point where, after dawn broke and the thin fog lifted from the harbour, I began to wonder if he was dead.

'Eventually, a figure in a long, hooded overcoat shuffled towards the harbour and caught the interest of the men. We watched as it slowly approached the ship. Something about the figure gave me the shivers, but as First Mate I was the one who had to go down and see what it wanted.

'Well, it spoke to me and I almost died of fright on the spot. "Is she ready?" asked a voice from the shadows of the black hood, and I knew then that this shambolic figure was none other than Grice himself. Even though the voice had deepened, and become filled with gravel, there was no mistaking it. He looked like he'd put on a tremendous amount of weight, but with the coat and the darkness it was hard to see what was what, exactly.

'"She's ready, Captain," I said, stepping aside. Grice shuffled up the boarding planks and immediately went down into his cabin. The men stood on deck, looking at each other with fright.

The Indians disembarked and refused to board. I had to go down and argue with them for over twenty minutes, and in the end the only way they would rejoin the ship was under agreement that their wages would be doubled. We needed those Indians, we were lost without them. I had to agree to their terms, and I knew that at some point I would have to admit these terms to Grice.

'So we sailed, setting off on the last whaling trip I ever took. Right at the start I knew that we shouldn't have gone, but you can't put an end to your livelihood on the whim of a bad feeling.

'We took the usual route around the Horn, and for once the weather was reasonable. I've seen swells there the size of mountains, and have more than once been convinced of my imminent death. Many ships have gone down in those waters, and I've lost perhaps a dozen good friends there. This particular time, we were lucky, although the Third Mate fractured his arm when the swell pitched him into the tryworks, and he probably wouldn't see our luck in the same light as me. Still, it was nothing a sling and time wouldn't fix.

'Within two months we were back in our favourite hunting grounds. In all that time, Grice hadn't ventured onto the deck. I had to have some dealings with him, and was the only crewman to venture down to his cabin. He kept it in darkness and spoke to me from the shadows. It was a strange business, there was no doubt. I knew, by this time, that there was something seriously wrong with him. His unwillingness to show himself was testament to that, and his voice was becoming harder to understand as the weeks passed.

'We dealt with the normal business of running the ship. He asked our bearings every time we spoke, and made me give him a full report of the happenings on deck, however trivial. He seemed lucid and fully in control of the ship, but it was clear that something was on his mind. As the weeks passed, the pauses dotting his speech grew longer, and he began to sound distracted. Then, one day, he said things that were to disturb me a great deal.

'"I can hear them," he said.

'I naturally assumed he was talking about the crew. Although his presence penetrated every fibre of the ship, the men were now used to working without Grice overseeing them, and had settled about their business in a manner that was somewhat cheerier than normal. Whales were killed without any ugly business involving axes, and the corpses were dealt with quickly and efficiently. After each batch of processing, the decks and the rest of the ship were thoroughly cleaned and the men relaxed for a short while, letting their hair down, so to speak. Some of them had even taking to dancing a jig in celebration of each kill, a new habit that had undoubtedly arisen solely because Grice, a somewhat dour and humourless bastard at the best of times, wasn't on hand to reprimand them for their foolishness. And also, perhaps, because as First Mate I had taken it upon myself to be a little more generous with the rum rations than usual, which I had admitted to Grice and he had let continue.

'It was this that I thought Grice was referring to - the hard soles of the crew's footwear banging on the deck above Grice's cabin as they jigged.

'I'm sorry, Sir – I'll ask the men to stop their dancing.'

'"No, you fool! Not the men..... Them. The whales. I can hear the whales, in the deep. They're talking to each other."

'Now, it's not unusual to hear whales calling to each other, especially when you're below deck in moments of quiet. Water is a very good conductor of sound, and we all knew that the whales were capable of emitting some very strange noises. I was somewhat confused that Grice should have raised the subject – it was something that, perhaps, a new cabin boy would have noted on his first voyage, not something a seasoned Captain would have mentioned.

'"Let's hope they aren't telling each other that we're about the business of hunting them," I joked.

'"That's exactly what they're doing," he said.

'"Sir?"

'"Listen to me, damn it! How many times....? I hear the whales talking to each other. I understand what they're saying."

'You hear a thing like that, and hear the conviction in the voice that's saying it, you quickly realise that the owner of that voice is insane. Grice had been halfway there anyway, but this development made the hairs on my neck stand on end. Remember, we were weeks from the nearest landfall, and completely at his mercy.

'"Captain Grice, Sir," I said. "I hope you'll forgive me for what I'm about to say, but it seems that you aren't quite yourself. As First Mate, I have a duty to enquire about your condition – the safety of the men is paramount."

'A low, guttural laugh came from the shadows. My blood felt like Arctic ice-water, and it was all I could do not to flee back to the deck. I heard various shuffling and scrapings in the darkness, the sound of movement.

'"Light a candle," he said.

'My hands were shaking as I lit a match and held it to a candle on the small table in the centre of the room. The wick caught and the flame guttered a fraction before settling. A dim yellow light brought the rest of the cabin into view.

'I actually cried aloud with horror at the sight of him. Grice was a hideous, deformed version of his former self, and he had doubled in weight. His clothes were in tatters and his overcoat was the only thing that offered cover. And his face....! It was a swollen, lumpy mess, with eyes bulging in their sockets.

'I backed away from him. I was terrified.

'"What has happened to you?" I asked.

He looked at the floor and breathed heavily for a few moments.

'"That thing we found...." he said finally, scratching at a bloated cheek with fingers that seemed to be fusing together. "That thing did this to me. It is me. It became me. I kept it in my house, thinking it safe, not knowing what was to come. It had the bathtub to itself, and a daily change of fresh water.

'"Bess was afraid of it, and begged me to destroy it but I wouldn't listen. She took to barring the bedroom door from the inside, and I laughed at her foolishness. She tried to convince me that this thing was dangerous, but it seemed content enough in the tub, and I came to think of it as something of a pet, even though my end purpose was to sell it, and made certain enquiries to that end. Barnum himself was interested in making the trip up from New York to see it.

'"In the meantime, I studied it. Up close, it was a disgusting creature, a fleshy mass of something jelly-like and yet solid at the same time. There were veins beneath the surface, evidence of a rudimentary blood system, and perhaps a heart. It had that one white eye, large and unblinking, and many times I tried to communicate with it in an effort to determine a level of intelligence. It would fix me with that terrible eye and pulse with life, and though I knew it harboured some secret intelligence it ignored my attempts at communication.

'"It seemed ancient, to me, as old as the Earth itself, old enough to have scoured the oceans for aeons, looking for things to host it. That must have been the key to its survival, for in all the time I kept it not once did it accept food of any kind. It grew smaller, as though shrivelling through a lack of sustenance, and as the days went by it seemed to grow more agitated.

'"Barnum sent word that he had spent many thousands of dollars on the complete skeleton of a sabre-toothed tiger, and he was very apologetic but my creature no longer held any interest for him. I grew despondent and my thoughts turned to killing it. And then, suddenly, my sister-in-law died in childbirth and Bess went to Halifax for a few days to attend to the aftermath. I was left alone with the creature, and my lax attitude to personal safety was my downfall.

'"I didn't bar the bedroom door, and one night I awoke to find the thing on top of me – somehow, it had made its way out of the tub, across the landing and into the bedroom, and had climbed onto the bed, pinning me with its weight. I couldn't get it off! It had spread itself out, pinning my arms by my sides, and nothing I did would shift it from the bed. Only my head was out of the covers, and for a few moments that milky eye hovered right above my face, staring down at me, unblinking.

'"There was no mistaking it, this thing was an intelligent creature, a sentient being with an agenda. It forced its way into my mouth. I bit off great chunks and spat them out, but it simply kept coming and overwhelmed me, pouring itself down my throat. I couldn't breathe, I couldn't move. I felt it travel down my windpipe, down through my oesophagus and into my lungs, into my stomach. This thing invaded me. By the time I could get my breath, every last bit of it had disappeared inside me! It sounds impossible, but I speak the truth. Look at me! And there it remains, inside me."

'He finished speaking and once again looked at the floor. In the dim light, I thought I saw a single teardrop fall, but I could have been mistaken. I had listened to his story with a growing sense of horror, considering it the rant of a madman and a reflection of Grice's current state of mind. But, the fact was, something terrible had happened to Grice, and his physical appearance was evidence of some massive trauma, of some mechanism of change within.

'"Did you consult a doctor?" I asked.

'"Three of them. They didn't believe me. One tried to put a tube in my throat and the thing reacted with such violence it almost killed me."

'"Maybe we should let the Indians examine you," I said.

'"The Indians? For the love of God, man, why?"

'"They know about these things," I said, not knowing if this was true or not. All I wanted was to get out of that cabin, and any excuse would do.

'"Whether they do, or not, it would kill me, I'm certain. For the moment, we should continue as normal, until I know what it wants. It must have had a reason for using my body."

'I stood there, unsure about how to proceed.

"'Why are you here?' I asked at last. "Why another expedition, in the state you're in?"
'He looked up at me, his distorted face bathed in a genuine sadness. I almost felt sorry for him.
'"Killing whales is the only thing I know. I'm dying, that much is obvious. This will be my last voyage. I would like to die with a lance in my hand, my body soaked with the warm blood of a whale. Do you understand?"
'I didn't understand, not one bit.
'"I want you to speak to the men," he said, his voice suddenly clear and firm. "Prepare them."
'"For what, Sir?"
'"For me. I need to come up to the deck. I've been rotting away in this cabin and I need fresh air, I need to feel the weight of a lance in my hand before I forget how to kill whales. I want the men warned about how I look. I do not want them to panic."
'"Are you sure this is a good idea? I don't wish to sound callous, but the sight of you like this will unsettle them a great deal."
'"Then let them be unsettled! Have you not grown used to the sight of me already?"
'"No, Sir. Not really."
'"Ha! Me neither."

'There was an air of bitter resignation in his voice, and also a great deal of fear. A few months ago, I would have thought it impossible for a man like Grice to be afraid of anything – I'd seen him standing atop thrashing whales in seas of mountainous waves, as dangerous a position as it's possible to be in this life, with little thought to his own safety. But he knew he was dying, and the definitive knowledge of one's own mortality brings a different kind of fear, a terror of certain death, a doom that is inescapable. It was coming for him, and he was perhaps afraid of meeting his maker. Grice had lived a life filled with terrible carnage and maybe he thought there would be some sort of Reckoning for that.

'"I'll have words with the men," I said, welcoming my chance to escape. I left him to his thoughts and rejoined the men on deck.

'I had been down in the cabin a long time, and my emergence into the sunlight made me stop and turn my face to the sun, eyes closed, basking in the heat and light. Something about my countenance attracted the attention of the men – there was probably a tangible air of relief surrounding me. They all cast glances my way, curious. The Second Mate walked over and stood next to me.

'"How is the old coot?" he asked.

'"You'll see for yourself, soon enough. He'll be coming out on deck shortly."

'He looked around in a panic, ensuring everything was shipshape. He needn't have worried – the lack of Grice's presence on a daily basis hadn't led to any slippage in efficiency or standards – all men did their job as surely as if Grice had loomed over them, inspecting every action. Like I said, they already feared him. Surely that fear would only deepen once Grice dragged himself out into the light.

'"Listen," I added. "He doesn't look the same. We need to gather the men and tell them that Grice now looks…. different."

'"How different?"

'"His physical appearance has altered tremendously. He no longer looks like the Grice we knew, but underneath he's exactly the same. This is what we need to make the men understand."

'So we drew the men into a short conference, warning them of what to expect. They looked incredulous, and then wary, unsure of this new business. The Indians remained grim-faced but their eyes betrayed their inner thoughts – they were terrified. Despite my outward confidence, I felt exactly the same.

'Not long after the men had resumed their duties, Grice heaved himself up the galley stairs leading to the deck. He was dressed in his long overcoat and hood, his face and body out of view, but every last man could see that he had grown enormously. He stood on the deck, commanding the attention of the crew by the sheer force of his presence.

'For a long time he stood there in silence, breathing heavily, no doubt drawing fresh air into his lungs and acclimatising himself to the light after so long in his quarters. The men had by now abandoned any pretence of working, and simply stared.

'Suddenly, he took off his coat and flung it aside. There was a collective gasp from the crew, followed by the murmuring of their agitated voices. In broad daylight, Grice looked even worse than the vision I'd seen by candle-light in his cabin. His body was bloated and mis-shapen, covered with lumps, and could barely be contained by his splitting clothes. His face was wrecked, distorted out of shape. His skin, what could be seen, was grey and ashen. Panting, he looked at all of us in turn.

'"What devilry is this?" shouted the Second Mate.

'"Not devilry," I told them all, "but simply misfortune. Captain Grice has been taken with a parasitic disease. Do not worry yourselves, it is not catching."

'The men were clearly not happy at this manifestation of Grice, in their midst. The Indians had removed themselves aft, conferring in hushed voices. The rest of the men, stood where they were, uncertain.

'"Nothing has changed!" I shouted. "We hunt whales, as usual."

'Grice shuffled to the centre of the deck.

'"I am your Captain!" he shouted. "This is my ship! Do not forget it! Now get back to work!" At this, any notion the men had that this strange figure was not Captain Grice was dispelled, yet still they paused, hesitant to surrender to this new notion of normality. Grice turned and slowly shuffled back down to his cabin, and I was left alone at the centre of the deck, with everybody now staring at me.

'"You heard the man," I shouted. "Back to work!"

'Within moments, they were back at their stations.

# FOUR

**Four**

'During the following week, we caught three baleen whales and narrowly missed catching a young bull sperm. Grice took no part in the slaughter, preferring instead to stand on deck and watch. Although the men were now slowly becoming used to Grice being in their midst, they were wary of him, and avoided him where possible.

'The sea air appeared to offer no rejuvenating qualities for Grice. In fact, it seemed to have the opposite effect, because his condition seemed to worsen. If anything, he grew even bigger, and soon resembled a man of perhaps twenty-five stone. His skin, grey like pale granite, came out in splotches of white. His throat grew in size disproportionately to the rest of him, and bulged as though filled with liquid, and this made his voice become even more low and rasping. I struggled to understand him clearly.

'"I hear them," he kept saying to himself, over and over. "Down there, talking to each other. They know I'm here."

'Not long after Grice came out into the light, so to speak, the night terrors began. During the hours of darkness, when the ship was silent save for the creak of old timber and the gentle slapping of the waves against the hull, the most unholy noises began to emerge from Grice's cabin: screams, shouts, and long howls that descended into deep, resonant moans.

'They were the most terrifying sounds I have ever heard, even worse than those made by the whales as we were killing them. The crew gathered on deck, out of their minds with fright. The sounds coming from Grice's cabin were inhuman. They echoed around the hold of the ship, and rang out into the night sky. You would have been able to hear them for miles.

'I calmed the men as best as I could, and told them that it was merely a symptom of his condition.

'"You have to go down there," said the Second Mate.

'Naturally, I argued against it, but in the end they all made me do it. That walk down to his cabin was the longest of my life. I could hardly climb down the stairs because my legs were shaking so much. A belching sound made my hair stand on end, so powerful that I heard things falling from their shelves in the galley.

'"Captain Grice, Sir?" I said in a quiet voice, standing outside his cabin door. I was hoping he wouldn't hear me, so I could retreat. There was a groan from inside. Cautiously, I opened the door and peered in. The room was completely dark. The smell emanating from inside made me flinch. I almost ran screaming when Grice spoke.

'"They are coming for me," he said, his voice barely legible.

'I stepped inside the cabin, lighting a match. There was a fresh candle on the table, and I focussed on getting the flame to catch. As the room lit up in the weak glow cast off by the flame, I looked across at Grice. He was virtually unrecognisable.

'Even as I watched, he flinched with a violent spasm, threw back his head and let out the most horrendous screeching sound. I almost fainted with fear, and my skin was alive with goosebumps. I can still hear that sound in my nightmares sometimes, even now, thirty years later.

'The cabin descended into silence.

'"Who is coming?" I asked.

'"The whales. It's calling them."

'"It?"

'"The thing inside me. I now know what it wants. I thought it was my decision to come out on one last voyage," said Grice, his voice slow and even. "But I was wrong. It made me come. These noises I make, it's the thing calling to them, in their own language. I have no control over it. It tells the whales I'm here, and they want their revenge for all the things I have done. But all of us are naught but pawns! It wants to get back to the ocean, do you understand? It wants to get at those whales, more than those whales want to get at me."

'"Captain Grice, Sir....."

'"Listen to me, damn it!" he shouted, his voice distorting as it increased in volume. "I'm a weak host, and it needs something stronger! It's desperate to get back inside one of those whales, to continue its vile business! And they come, not knowing the truth of what calls them!"

'The parasite inside him, the disease or whatever it was, had taken the last of his sanity. Clearly, there was nothing I could do for him.

'"You need rest, Sir. Is there anything I can get for you?" I asked, backing to the doorway. "Some fresh water?"

'"You don't believe me." he said.

'I couldn't lie to him, so I said nothing.

'"My lance," he said, a flatness in his voice. "Have it ready for the morning."

'I left the cabin and closed the door. Now I was faced with the task of telling the men that our Captain was probably going to be incapacitated in his duties for the remaining duration of the voyage. Whatever madness had hold of Grice, it was filling his head with preposterous ideas, and I grew concerned about the safety of the crew. His condition was worsening, and I already knew beyond doubt that Grice was a man capable of extreme violence. And this maniac wanted me to prepare his lance? Much as I detested the idea, I began to admit to myself that I would soon have to take full control of the ship. For the foreseeable future, I would have to take on the mantle of Captaincy.

'With a heavy heart, I climbed back onto the deck, wondering how I should put my thoughts to the crew. They didn't even notice my arrival. They were all, to a man, standing on port and starboard, looking down at the waters. I called over the Second Mate.

'"What is going on here?" I asked him. "Why are the men not at their stations?"

"Whales, Sir," he said. "As many as I've ever seen in one place, all at once. They've surrounded the ship."

'I ran to starboard and looked down. As far as the eye could see, enormous black shapes cut through the still waters, circling the Nautilus. Grice's words echoed in my head:

'"They are coming for me."

**FIVE**

## Five

'All night they circled the ship. Amongst the inky waters, these leviathans moved gracefully, with only the occasional spray from a blowhole breaking the silence. The sea was calm, and a supernatural peace had settled over everything, at least that's how it seemed to me.

'The men whispered amongst themselves, watching the spectacle, afraid of what it might mean. If things were different, we might have been busy with the business of hunting, for this was a bounty we were unlikely to see ever again, but nobody made a move. The boats remained tied up against the ship. The Indians left their harpoons untouched.

'We waited.

'Just before dawn, there came a sudden loud belching noise from Grice's cabin. At once, the whales stirred into a commotion of activity, spraying and snorting, picking up speed. One or two of them knocked against the ship with enough force to knock men off their feet. The whales circled faster, and closer, and one of them sent up a high-pitched keening sound, the like of which I'd never heard before.

'We all turned at the sound of Grice, shuffling and heaving himself up the steps onto the deck. His transformation from a man into an unrecognisable mountain of grey flesh was virtually complete. He staggered forward on hideously deformed legs, and the men cleared out of his path, terrified. He fixed his gaze down onto the sea, and made a deep groaning sound. The whales responded, all at once. A chorus of moans filled the air. For all intents and purposes, it appeared that they were attempting conversation with Grice. It sounds impossible, but that's how it looked to us crew.

'The Indians were babbling in their own tongue, as frightened as I'd ever seen them. The Third Mate was sitting on deck, his back to the tryworks, head in his hands. He had given up in despair.

'"What is happening here?" I demanded of Grice.

'Slowly, he turned and looked at me. He opened his mouth and spoke, but they were words I couldn't understand, rasping words, twisted into some unrecognisable language. I backed away, horrified, and he turned his attention back to the water. He howled, lifting his mis-shapen head back to expose his bulging throat, and the whales below responded with howls of their own. One of them rammed the ship and sent us sprawling.

'The Second Mate ran over to me.

'"They want the Captain," he said. "It's obvious. Give him to them!"

'I'd known this man for over twenty years, all of them served by his side under the captaincy of Grice. I knew that he had the utmost respect for Grice, and I'd never heard him say a bad word against him, which was unusual because once ashore the rest of us all discussed Grice's antics with a mixture of amusement and horror. He must have been terribly afraid to speak such a thought aloud, knowing that I, as his superior, would be bound to take such mutinous talk with a view to having him arrested. But I stayed where I was, paralysed with indecision. The thought had already crossed my mind of its own accord, but I couldn't let this be known amongst the crew.

'"Hold your tongue!" I warned him.

'But I thought it through. Whatever that parasite was, it had destroyed Grice, for he was clearly dying. I doubted that he would make the journey through to the end, and that at some point he would be going overboard anyway, buried at sea forever. But could I order such an action whilst he was still alive?

'And was this strange turn of events really down to Grice, and his insane theory?

'He had hunted whales for the better part of forty years, and must have killed many hundreds – each time lancing them from the boat and, unless the seas were exceptionally rough, stepping out onto the whales to finish them with his customary axe attack. During these decades, other whales must have seen Grice about the business of killing. Was it possible that he had become known to them?

'Did they afford him legendary status in their kingdom? I had helped carve up enough whale heads in my time, and I knew that the size of a whale brain is enormous. Did that equate to intelligence? Were these creatures actually capable of remembering, and identifying a particular individual from our human race?

'Would it be that great a leap to imagine the possibility?

'Not so, I thought. These things had come for Grice, that much was evident by simply looking at the sea below, and by hearing their grunts, moans and howls when responding to those of Grice. But, there was another thought, and perhaps one more prescient – maybe Grice had also been right about the thing inside him, calling out to the whales with its own agenda. We had found the damned thing inside a whale – was it at all possible that Grice had spoken the truth, that it was merely using him with the sole aim of returning to its natural domain? Who knows how long that thing had lived? In all possibility, it had been killing whales since the very dawn of time, and may even have been a more fearsome predator than Grice himself!

'Either way, tipping Grice overboard would solve the matter, but I couldn't bring myself to do it, not whilst he bore the last remaining vestiges of humanity. It would be murder. Had I known what was about to happen, I wouldn't have hesitated. My decision caused the deaths of a great many men, and I'm sure they will be waiting for me when my time is come.

'So we waited, helpless as events unfolded. The 'conversation' between Grice and the whales grew ever louder and more fierce. The sea frothed with the agitation of the whales as they circled around the Nautilus with increasing speed. One or two lifted themselves from the waters, high until they were completely airborne, and level with the deck of the ship. A living whale out of water is a most unnatural sight to behold, and one that reduces even the bravest of men to a quivering wreck. One of those airborne whales looked into my eyes, and I swear I saw Nature's purest manifestation of rage. They landed in the water, throwing up waves that engulfed the ship, soaking the men and even washing one overboard. We ran to the starboard and watched in horror as our cook was snagged between a set of massive jaws and broken in two.

'Grice shuffled over to the harpoons and held one aloft, throwing back his head and letting out a great belching sound. He held it up for the whales to see, howling his anger at them, and turned back to face the horrified crew. With great effort, he uttered the last words he would ever speak in our language: "KILL... THEM....!" Even then, his one thought was that of killing whales. He attempted to hurl the harpoon down towards the black shapes in the water, and that was the moment our fate was sealed. The harpoon missed, for Grice was now far too bulky and clumsy to wield it in any dangerous fashion, but the whales had witnessed his intent and it sent them into a frenzy. Upon some unknown signal, they scattered away from the ship, heading out to sea in all directions before turning back to face us. Then, as we watched, they began their attack.

'The first came at us so hard that it knocked itself out cold, headbutting the side of the Nautilus with enough force to shunt the entire ship sideways. It rolled over and drifted away, either unconscious or perhaps dead, but the next whale was already coming for us. The Second Mate screamed.

'The whale hammered into the side of the ship and we heard the sound of breaking wood. I shouted at some of the men to go below decks and prepare for bailing duty, and ordered the Indians to grab their harpoons. They were too afraid to move, and I had to run over and shout at them, so close that my face was inches from theirs, covering them with my spit. They were stirred into action, but we were all sent flying onto our backsides by a third strike at the ship. At the starboard, Grice was standing there watching, his gelatinous blob of a body shaking with maniacal laughter.

'There was no time to deal with him, and little point in trying – he had incited the war and it was now too late to stop it. Instead, I focussed on commandeering the men, getting them to aim the harpoons and lances at the approaching whales with the intention of letting them see that attacking us was futile. But it was far from futile, and they knew it. From above, our weapons were useless, even if they struck home. Unless you hit the lungs, such injuries only make the whales angrier. They started coming at us in twos, and I knew that the Nautilus, and all on her, were doomed.

'It was a very short and one-sided war. A whaling ship, however majestic and seaworthy, is no match for a direct attack by such angry, enormous creatures. As whales crashed into the ship, men fell from the rigging into the waters, lost in a commotion of spray, some of them crushed and killed by the whipping of leviathan flukes. Each successive barrage weakened the ship until it could hold out no more. They sank her. There was small, grim satisfaction in knowing that the whale to completely breach the hull was stuck fast and went down with the ship. Men were thrown overboard and others had no choice but to jump. We were floating about in the turbulent waters, smashed by the whales and grabbing anything we could to stay afloat. The Nautilus went down in a matter of minutes, and, sensing their victory, the whales backed off and stopped their attack.

'I could see Grice, a short distance away, floating without the aid of any flotsam, his eyes wide with terror. Nearby, two of the Indians clung to an empty barrel that had somehow made its way out of the hold. I saw more perhaps a dozen bodies floating in various states of death and dismemberment, the crew of the Nautilus, men whom I had sailed with for many years. Close by, I recognised the corpse of the Second Mate. From what I could tell, only four of us had survived the attack.

'I expected the whales to come and finish us off. Instead, they dispersed, and circled at a distance. Now that Grice was in the water, their rage had turned to fear. They knew that something was wrong. Only one returned, an old bull that was perhaps sixty feet in length, covered in barnacles with a lance sticking out of its back. It swam close to Grice and appeared to sniff at him, and with a shriek it suddenly turned and fled. It knew! I tell you, it knew, at that moment, the truth of the matter. And then, so did I. However much that whale wanted Grice, it knew that the thing was inside him, waiting for its moment.'

The old man stopped talking and took a sup at his beer. He looked so very sad, fragile and old and nearing the end of his days. His remaining eye was watery with the memories, and for a moment I thought he might break down and cry. But he took stock of himself, finished his drink and set about filling his pipe once more.

'So what happened next?' I asked him, eager to hear the outcome of this strange tale.

'Well,' said the old man, 'we must have drifted for days. A storm caught us and the Indians were separated, and were never heard from again. I tried to stay close to Grice, but I didn't want to get too close, and by the time they found us we must have been the better part of half a mile apart.'

'Who found you?' I asked.

'The Misquam, a whaler from Nantucket. They told me that an old bull whale with a lance in its back had led them right to us. Well, to Grice actually.'

'So they picked you up and brought you home?' I said. 'That was a stroke of luck.'

'Not quite, lad. There's no sympathy aboard whaling ships, and there was no way they would abandon their own voyage simply to give me a ride home. I was appropriated into their crew, demoted down to Fourth Mate because that was the only position available to me. It was another year before my feet touched soil.'

'What did they do with Grice?'

'They harpooned him.'

'They did what?'

'They thought he was a calf whale,' he said, smiling ruefully. 'The old bull disappeared and at the sight of Grice, they wasted no time in sending out the boats and hunting him down. I told you, there's no sympathy from whalers, and even a young calf will yield a few barrels of oil. In fact, they even dealt with Grice before they could be bothered to come and pluck me out of the water.'

'I swam towards the ship and by the time I was halfway there, the boats had rowed back and the crew were already lifting Grice out of the water. His clothing had completely fallen away, and all that was left of him was a bulk of grey, marbled flesh.

They must have realised that it was one of the strangest-looking whales ever created, but in the heat of the retrieval nobody had looked too closely. They had him up against the side of the ship, cutting into him with the flensing spades before they realised it wasn't a whale at all. I could hear his screams from where I watched in shock, treading water. He was half-butchered and certainly dead when they let him go, and the mess had brought the sharks. I managed to attract the attention of the ship and they finally sent one of the boats out to pick me up.

'And, at the end, even the sharks were afraid of the thing inside Grice. As we watched from the boat, Grice's body collapsed inwardly, and a black mass forced its way out through one of the wounds and slid into the water. The crew of the Misquam cried out in alarm, and the sound brought the milky eye of the creature into view as it looked up at the ship and studied them for a moment. Then, with a high-pitched shriek of triumph, the thing dived below the surface and vanished. Only then did the sharks approach and attack the corpse of Grice with a ferocity that was terrifying. I couldn't get aboard the Misquam quickly enough, I tell you.

'All that happened thirty years ago. It was the last time I was ever out at sea. Since I came back onto dry land, I never left it again.'

We sat there in silence, and the old man looked out through the window at the blurry landscape of New Bedford's harbour. He was deep in thought, and I sat there thinking over his story. There was a certain symmetry to the universe, and the whales had got their revenge after all. Grice had met the end he deserved. All men do, one way or the other.

The tavern door opened and in stepped a young man of about thirty. There was a resemblance to the old man who had talked my ears off for the better part of an hour.

'My son,' said the old man, disturbed from his reverie. 'Here, John – I have a passenger for you.'

'Not a passenger,' I corrected. 'I'm prepared to work.'

The man walked over and shook my hand, and smiled warmly.

'Let me get you a drink,' I said. 'And your throat must be dry as a bone by now,' I added, looking at the old man. 'He has some wild stories, your father.'

'Ah, he hasn't been telling that one about the whale again, has he?'

'How did you know?'

'It's the only story he has – he tells it to anyone who'll listen.'

'It's a good story!' protested the old man.

I ordered a round of drinks, paid the miserable, oafish barman, and sat down again. It occurred to me that I'd listened to the entire story on the pretence that I'd hear about how the old man lost his eye, and that loss was still a complete mystery.

'So how did you lose your eye?' I asked him.

'I have a brother in Fairhaven who farms goats. He wanted help milking them a few summers ago, and as I was behind one of them it lashed out and kicked me right in the eye.'

'So, nothing to do with the whale?'

'No. Nothing to do with the whale.'

# BONUS STORY

# LOOKING INTO A FURNACE

## STEVE ROACH

## Looking into a Furnace

Cal called in the afternoon and asked if I was going to town that night. Of course, I'd said, why would this Saturday be any different? He thought I was seeing some bird and the truth is I was supposed to but she'd blown me out earlier in the week. I couldn't tell him that though, he'd tell the others and that'd be it for the next few weeks, endless piss-taking. So I told him I'd fucked her off for being too needy and I'd meet him in the Clock for one on the way.

When I arrived, the rest of the gang was already there. Stevie and Dobb were a couple of pints in already. They were both big lads and I'd seen them sink twenty each in a day before so a couple wouldn't even wet their throats.

"Alright?" asked Cal, slapping me on the shoulder. He moved to one side and I saw a fresh pint waiting for me. He's a good man, is Cal. They all are. They're the brothers I never had. We'd all been through a few scrapes together, down the years, and we were still standing. I couldn't ask for better mates.

We knocked back the drinks and started walking into town. We were about a mile off and the walk usually took twenty minutes or so. Stevie would inevitably need a piss along the way and would end up in someone's garden hosing down their roses. On the way back, gone midnight, he'd stop in a garden (sometimes even the same garden) and do it again. A couple of times he'd even put his half-eaten kebab on someone's wall whilst he'd stopped to take a shit. Disgusting, I know, but funny when one of us sends him the YouTube link the next day after a bit of covert filming on a mobile.

Halfway there, we were approached by a young Japanese woman. She was holding a wireless microphone and a drone hovered over her right shoulder.

"Hello gentlemen," she said in a bright voice. "Do you want to be on tv?"

Dobb stepped forward to speak with her, which I didn't think was a good idea. Dobb wasn't much keen on Orientals. He wasn't much keen on anybody who wasn't white and British. He's always been that way. At school, he did himself a tattoo on the webbing between his thumb and index finger of his left hand, using biro ink and a compass. He drew a swastika and although it's faded now it's still obvious. It's cost him at least a couple of jobs, as far as I know, probably more. I mean, who wants a racist working for them? What the interviewers wouldn't know about Dobb is that he has another, much larger and more professionally done tattoo of a swastika covering his back, along with a portrait of Hitler.

"Is that a camera?" he asked, jabbing a thick finger up towards the drone. Her lower jaw almost dislocated itself with a huge grin and she nodded vigorously. "Are we on telly right now?" he asked.

"This just preliminary filming," she said. Her high-pitched voice and fixed grin made her seem like a maniac struggling to control herself. "Tv later."

"What kind of show is it?" I asked.

"Game show. Big prize!"

I looked at the others and shrugged.

"Fuck it," I said. "Why not?"

"Have we got time for it?" asked Stevie. I knew what he was thinking. Stevie's idea of a good night out involved drinking as much as possible, getting into a fight with someone and then finishing off with a curry or a kebab. Quite a schedule and Saturday night was easily the most important part of his week. He was worried that if we did this for a couple of hours we might not have time to fit everything else in.

"Relax," I said. "It'll be fun. And we might win something."

He grudgingly relented. I turned back to the woman.

"We're in," I said.

"Good news!" she squealed and turned to look up at the drone. "Contestants ready!" she cried, throwing her arms up for dramatic effect.

A black van appeared as if from nowhere and pulled up next to us. The side door opened and the woman pointed at the dark interior. It didn't look that inviting.

"What prizes did you say?" I asked her.

"Yes, many prize! Big prize! In, in!"

With a sigh, Stevie poked his head inside for a quick look around and clambered in. The rest of us followed. With a pitter-patter of stiletto heels on paving slabs, the woman ran over and slammed the door, leaving us in darkness for a few moments before a dim red light came on. There were no seats so we were sitting on the floor. A dull rumble swept through the van as the engine started and we felt ourselves being driven away.

"Are we sure this is a good idea?" asked Dobb.

"It doesn't matter," said Cal, his face a Devil mask in the red light. Let's just see what happens."

"If I'd known I was going to be on the telly I'd have made more of an effort," said Stevie, combing over his fringe with a sweaty hand. "Fuckin' hot in here," he added as an afterthought.

We were driven for about ten minutes, by which time I was beginning to lose my patience. Just as I was about to bang on the side of the van, it turned a sharp corner and then rumbled up some sort of uneven road. We stopped shortly afterwards and someone came over and opened the side door.

We stepped out, shielding our eyes from the evening sun. We were parked in front of the biggest warehouse I'd ever seen.

"Follow me, please," said a small Japanese man with a clipboard. He led us to a door, which he opened and we all followed him through. We ended up in a brightly lit room. There was no furniture other than a table with a few shrink wrapped items on it.

"Please, change," said the man, pointing at the table. Stevie wandered over, picked one of the packets up and opened it. He was soon holding up a pair of white overalls. I looked around the room and noticed two cameras mounted to the walls.

"Are you going to record us getting changed?" I asked.

"No, no, not working," said the man. He was grinning like a Cheshire cat. I could tell he was lying as there were little red lights on them so even if we weren't being filmed we were probably being watched. What kind of tv programme was this, I wondered.

Stevie stripped down to his pants and put on the overalls. We did the same.

"No shoes!" said the man.

"Why not?" I asked.

"Ruin equipment!" he said. Reluctantly, we all took off our shoes. "Sock too!" he said.

Satisfied that we were ready, the man walked over to another door and motioned us through.

"Go to end," he said, still smiling. "Wait."

When we'd filed through he closed the door behind us, leaving us alone.

"This is getting a bit weird," said Cal. "I've half a mind to tell 'em to go fuck themselves and get out of here. I'm telling you, these prizes better be worth it."

"I think it's going to be something like Total Wipeout," said Stevie.

"More like Takeshi's Castle," said Dobb. "With all these Japs knocking about."

We followed the corridor to another room. In the distance we heard a series of dull thuds. They were powerful enough to cause the thin metal walls of the corridor to buzz. Boom, Boom! There was a gap of perhaps two seconds before another two thudding sounds. It continued, forming a regular pattern.

We came to another room and were surprised to see a load of people already in there. Nobody was talking. I looked at them. Everyone here was male and aged between late teens and perhaps late fifties. A few had tattoos on their faces and necks. They all turned and looked us over. There was one guy I had to look twice at, a big bastard with close cropped ginger hair and a wonky eye. I thought I knew him from somewhere but the context of meeting him under these strange circumstances was throwing me off. I was about to turn and quietly converse with the others when a television screen burst into life.

"Hello contestants!" said a woman in a pink dress. She looked insanely happy and I recognised her as the woman who had approached us on the street and got us into this thing. "Congratulation on reach first stage. Begin in two minute."

The camera panned back from her a little and we could see that she also had bare feet. There were cartoon bugs crawling around on the floor beneath her. Squealing, she lifted up her feet and did a little dance. Bugs exploded beneath her. "Mashee-mashee!" she cried, laughing.

"What the fuck?" said one of the other guys in the room. He sounded like he was all out of patience. The air was getting tense.

The woman on the screen was replaced with a countdown.

"What do we have to do?" asked Cal. We were still in our own little sub-group.

"Looks like we have to squash some shit," said Stevie. "Maybe they're counting how many cockroaches we can kill or something."

"I don't like it," I said. "Something about this feels wrong."

We waited and watched the countdown pass the minute marker. With thirty seconds to go, everyone in the room jumped as three metal stutters on the back wall slid open and shadowy figures stood there watching us. It was hard to tell if they were real or just cardboard cut-outs – they didn't move an inch.

Cal touched my arm.

"They have baseball bats," he said, his voice quiet. I took a good look and saw that he was right. I felt my stomach sink a little.

On the screen, the counter dropped below twenty seconds.

"Hey, guys!" I called and a few heads turned in my direction. At this point the room was filled with men who were either bemused at what was happening, curious about any particular prizes that might be up for grabs, or frustrated and angry. The counter dropped to fifteen.

"What?" shouted the big ginger bastard.

"These guys..." I said, nodding at the shadowy figures.

I saw his eyebrows rise as he noticed that the figures were armed. "What the-"

His voice was cut off by the blare of a klaxon. A number of things seemed to happen at once. Beneath the television screen, a door opened into a wide corridor. LED's dotted the walls and flashed like runway lights, drawing us forward. Behind us, the shadowy figures stepped into the room and started swinging their bats and attacking us. I saw one guy's head rupture with a spray of blood as a bat connected with his skull and he dropped like a sack of shit.

"Run!" I shouted at the others.

Terrified now, unable to comprehend what the hell was really going on, I knew that we had to get away from the fuckers with the bats. We burst through the doorway and started running. The floor crunched beneath my feet and I had to swat things from the air with my hands. Then I noticed the sharp pains in the soles of my feet and a quick look down confirmed how far this madness was going – the floor was covered with wasps and we were running over them and getting stung repeatedly.

"Mashee-mashee!" screeched a voice, overpoweringly loud from unseen speakers.

Behind, someone was calling my name. I couldn't tell if it was Cal or Stevie – the voice was high-pitched with panic and I was too busy dealing with my own thoughts to try and focus on it. "Keep running!" I yelled, hoping this would be enough.

The booming sound was getting louder. Two loud bangs followed by a couple of seconds before it repeated. I roared with pain as another few stings burned into my feet and realised that wasps were starting to attack my arms and face as well. These bastards were going to pay for this – I didn't care what prizes were on offer, this was the most fucked-up game show I'd ever heard of.

At this point, I still had hopes of getting out of this experience alive. That changed as the corridor slowly curved and we entered a cavernous room and saw what was waiting for us.

Two rows of armed figures dressed in anti-riot gear lined the walls, one or two of them swinging baseball bats in readiness for an attack. I saw a flash of metal and realised that at least one of them was wielding a sword. Worse than this, the far end of the room contained a large opening, and this was the source of the terrible booming sounds. Above, in green neon lettering, was the word 'GOAL'. Blocking our way, two metal blocks came crashing down in quick succession – *Boom! Boom!* – before lifting up and falling down again. The front block came down first, followed by another behind it. But, as I watched, I then saw the second block drop before the first one. There was a pattern there I wouldn't have time to work out, or it could even have been random. Either way we were fucked.

Were we supposed to dash under them and hope we weren't crushed to death? My mind was still racing but I knew that the answer was yes. Whoever was running this madness was definitely prepared to kill us, for reasons I couldn't even begin to fathom. Had killed already, I guessed, as the man I saw dropped in the other room probably wouldn't have much of a skull left.

I'd slowed down without realising and Stevie, Dobb and Cal overtook me. They came to a halt and looked back. Their expressions were confused, terrified, and they looked like they were pleading with me to come up with some sort of explanation. I glanced around, trying to calculate an option. Any option. I had nothing.

The armed figures began converging on us.

One of the other contestants had kept running straight for the opening under the GOAL sign. I watched, fascinated, deliberately ignoring all of the other dangers, to see if he would make it. He ran at full sprint and ducked as he reached the opening, hoping his timing was right. The next second felt like it happened at a thousand miles an hour and lasted a hundred years at the same time. The first block came crashing down and obliterated him, smashing him between metal and the concrete floor in an explosion of gore. I nearly vomited as the block lifted up and I saw what was left.

"Fuck!" screamed Stevie.

I looked around. Some of the other contestants were trying to fight back against the men in riot gear. They were hopelessly ineffectual, their fists being no match for the bats and occasional sword. I saw on guy lose an arm, watched as it was sliced clean off and landed on the floor a few feet away. The guy didn't have time to even scream as a bunch of armed attackers piled into him and kept beating away with murderous intent.

They were going to kill us all.

We had to get out of this room.

"Move it!" I shouted, starting my run. If we were going to get out of this we had to go through those blocks. There might have been some other way but there was no time to assess the situation any further – if we didn't make a run for it in the next few seconds we wouldn't get a chance to do anything.

I developed tunnel vision and everything else was filtered out. All I could focus on was running forward and gauging the pattern of the blocks. Stevie pulled ahead of us all, his determined effort turning him into Usain Bolt, and as we drew nearer the opening I saw him drop to his knees and skid forward. For a moment I thought he might make it. He cleared the first block but the one behind caught him. Stevie was squashed like a bug, throwing out a curtain of blood and gristle.

As I reached the opening, the blocks were halfway up their rise. I threw myself forwards in a Superman dive, landing in Stevie's remains and using them as a lubricant to slide under both of the blocks. I kept my eyes closed until I thought I was through and then skidded to a halt and jumped to my feet. I was clear. As I turned back to look I saw Dobb clear the blocks, along with some guy we didn't know. Cal looked like he was going to make it, using the same technique I had, but the second block dropped down on him when he was only halfway through and as he opened his mouth to scream a torrent of his insides hosed the floor in front of us.

I ran back and grabbed his arms to pull him clear as the blocks rose again. The big ginger bastard came hurtling into him, bumping Cal's remains into the room but causing himself to stop. He looked at me with his one good eye, knowing he was about to die. There was no way he could get out from under there in time. In a final act of defiance – one that would burn itself in my brain until the time came for me to die – he formed a fist with his right hand and, as the blocks came down, roared and threw a punch up to meet them.

It was a pointless act, a futile gesture, but I could tell everything I needed to know about that man by that one simple snapshot of his willingness to go down fighting. And, at that moment, I remembered where I knew him from.

*Crystal Palace, 2013.*

A few more people made their way into this new room and then, suddenly, the blocks came down one last time and stopped. After the echoes had finished bouncing around the walls we were enveloped in a silence so complete that I actually forgot to breathe whilst I listened and waited for something else to happen.

"Congratulation! You success!"

The crazy woman in the pink dress was back, this time on a huge tv screen mounted on a stand in the otherwise empty room. I took a few moments to inspect the soles of my feet. They were throbbing with pain and already starting to swell. Considering I was still alive, I thought that I hadn't gotten off too badly.

Dobb limped over to me, his face red with anger.

"Some cunt's gonna get it for this," he snarled. He looked down at Cal's remains and I followed his gaze. An hour ago we were standing around in the pub, laughing and looking forward to the rest of the night. Now Stevie and Cal were both dead. It seemed incredible but it had happened and the nightmare was still happening. I briefly thought of Stevie's mother and then Cal's ex-girlfriend and daughter. Someone was going to have to explain this, as if anyone would believe it. I forced these thoughts from my mind and looked at Dobb.

"I knew one of the other guys," I told him.

"What do you mean?"

"The big ginger fuck. Manky eye."

"How do you know him?"

"He's dead, Dobb. We met him at Crystal Palace a few years ago. He was part of their crew."

Dobb looked back at me.

"I don't remember. Even so, it's just a coincidence, right?"

"I'm not sure. I don't think so."

"So these cunts knew who we were right from the get-go?" he asked.

"Possibly. I don't know."

In all, six of us made it through the blocks, including myself and Dobb. I took a good look around at the others but didn't recognise any of them. It would have been difficult anyway, considering we were all frightened out of our wits and covered in blood.

"Preparate round two!" screeched the Japanese woman from the tv.

"Fuck, there's more of this?" asked Dobb.

There was a hissing sound and we looked up to see plumes of mist billowing down from the ceiling. Now what? Were they gassing us?

"Find a way out of here," I told him. "Everyone! Listen to me! Find an exit and shout when you've found it!"

Nobody argued. We split up, running in different directions, each of us frantically hammering against the walls and looking for a doorway. All the while, the mist pumped into the room and descended. Soon we were all coughing.

I couldn't find a way out. Angry, thinking that these were my last seconds on Earth, I starting walking back towards the television set. If I wasn't getting out of here, I was going to smash that fucking thing to pieces. It would be nothing but a small act of defiance in the scale of things but it would have to be enough.

I didn't even get halfway. Coughing violently, my vision dimming, I collapsed to my knees and don't even remember toppling the rest of the way to the floor.

I was out cold.

*Crystal Palace, 2013.*
The train pulled into the station and we poured out of it, excited and half cut with cheap lager. The ride down had been a noisy one and the passengers had all moved to the back end of the train to get out of our way. Couldn't blame them, really. Still, that hadn't stopped one or two chopsing off at us and getting a good kicking in return.

These 'civilians' couldn't understand our world and viewed it with fear and contempt. They didn't understand what it was like to be part of a firm, how alive it made you feel. Normal life was an inconvenience, a mixture of chores and other mundane bullshit necessary to see us through to the next game where we could tool up and let loose and feel that beautiful adrenaline rush as the opposing crew ran towards us.

The Crystal Palace hoolies were called the Dirty 30. There were more than thirty of them, of course, and they were a tough crew. Most were. You didn't end up getting into this if you were a fucking weakling. You had to have bollocks the size of wrecking balls. Even though I've caved quite a few faces in over the years, I have the utmost respect for everyone I've maimed.

They were waiting for us at the station, as we'd expected. I turned to see Cal loading up with his knuckle dusters, one on each hand. He'd cracked dozens of skulls with those in the past. Stevie preferred a Stanley knife, he liked to rush in and start slashing. Once or twice we'd had to talk him out of bringing his favourite machete – I mean, there's got to be *some* restraint – but we all knew that one day he'd hide it on himself and bring it anyway. Dobb generally didn't bother with a weapon – being eighteen stone and boxing since he was a nipper meant he could handle himself very well using only his fists. He loved nothing more than cracking his knuckles against a stranger's nasal passages and rearranging their face before knocking them over and stamping on their head. As for me, I favoured an extendable steel baton, a handy little thing that locked into position at a foot long and extended your hitting range accordingly. With a baton, you could crack somebody's skull whilst they were swinging a blade and cutting nothing but air.

People screamed and dragged their children out of the way as our two firms converged on the platform and went at it. Even though it was an exceptionally violent pastime, I have to say that hooliganism provided me with the only peace I'd ever known. I'm not going to make excuses for my past, horrible though it was – I loved fighting and injuring people simply because I was a nasty cunt, regardless of any historic abuse or psychological trauma. In the middle of a good ruck, everything else faded away to nothing, every single problem, big or small, just disappeared for a while and I reached a kind of Zen state, a safe place where I could focus on nothing but my physicality and the ballet of violence playing out around me. You just don't get those moments of beauty anywhere else. To find true peace, you need to go to the extremes once in a while.

I lashed out at a few people, whipping the baton into their faces. Blood pumped through my veins and it felt like I was waking up after a hundred years of sleep. There was nothing on Earth like smashing people up, feeling them break under the power of the violence you gave out.

It worked both ways, that was the nature of these things. Within moments, I felt a hard crack against the side of my head and saw an explosion of lights before I fell to my knees. I readied myself for a blade or a boot but nothing came and when my vision cleared I saw Dobb standing over me with an arm extended to help me up. On the floor between us was a bloke lying face down, out of it.

"He hit you with a brick," said Dobb, heaving me up.

The side of my head was hot with pain and when I reached up to touch it my hand came away red.

"Thanks mate," I said, grimacing. He'd been there for me more than once, and vice versa. I really do mean it when I say these guys are my brothers. When you're in the trenches and the heat's really on, there's nobody else I'd want watching my back.

I gripped my baton and waded in for some more.

The battle lasted a good ten minutes before the police sirens started and we saw them coming through the station building. Some of the filth had been there for ages but they only come out to play when there's enough of them. Until they have decent numbers, they're happy to stand back and watch. And in that ten minutes, we'd all done enough damage to fill up the local casualty department. Blokes had been thrown off the platform onto the tracks and one had even been hoofed through a plate glass window. I hope somebody had filmed all of this so we could have a good laugh at the footage over a few beers later.

As the police piled out, both firms scattered and ran. Sometimes this gets reported as cowardice but nothing's further from the truth. We run so we can regroup and fight again. The next hotspot would be in the town so we made our way there in dribs and drabs, getting into minor scuffles with similarly displaced Palace goons.

When people read their newspapers the morning after a good ruck, they start up the usual discussions about what scum we are, how we're all mindless yobs. What these people fail to realise is that we're the backbone of society, the workers who keep the wheels turning. We're the mechanics, the cleaners, the chefs and estate agents, factory workers and waiters who keep the country running so all these moaning arseholes can continue to do whatever the fuck it is they do.

They don't realise that hooliganism has been a part of football for over a hundred years and always will be. Mostly young men, blowing off a bit of steam, there's no real harm in it. Civilians rarely get injured so I don't see what their fucking problem is. All these moaners who get on their high horses when we do a bit of fighting would soon change their tune if we ever got invaded. Do they think our army, with its diminished budgets and lack of equipment are going to save them? No, when things get ugly, and the Russians or the Germans are on our streets, it's going to be people like me who bear the brunt of the fighting and take these bastards down. We're the true saviours of Britain, make no mistake about it. And tear-ups on a Saturday afternoon are our way of staying sharp. People should be thanking us.

In the middle of town we met up with the rest of the stragglers and reformed our little army. The Dirty 30 weren't fully ready yet so we put a few shop windows through to keep the boredom level from dropping. As we stood around waiting, little figures hurried out of shop doorways and started pulling down their metal shutters. I saw a newsagent barricading up the front of his shop and briefly wished we'd waited to put the windows through so I could have nipped in and bought a packet of fags.

The two firms stood at each end of the main drag and slowly advanced. A big ginger man seemed to be leading up the opposition. He looked pretty handy, built like a brick shithouse and ready to cave in a few skulls. I moved to the front line of our group. I wanted a crack at that cunt before anyone else tagged him.

We were fifty yards away when some metal canisters landed in the street and started spewing out tear gas. In seconds, we were enveloped by a choking, eye-stinging cloud and we all started coughing and rubbing at our eyes. I heard someone shout as they were hit by some sort of projectile, followed by more shouts as stones and other missiles rained down on us.

"Get back!" somebody shouted. We retreated, stumbling our way through the gas, and were met by a wall of baton wielding filth with riot shields. That would be right. They waited until we were all incapacitated before giving us a good beating. And they beat the shit out of us that day, telling us never to return and packing us on a train home before the match had even started.

It was something of a downbeat end to the trip. When we got back home we had to get our frustration out by swarming a few of the city pubs, tearing it up a bit on our home turf and giving a few of the local lads a decent pasting. So not all bad.

It wasn't a particularly memorable day, not compared to some of our better outings, but one thing I did remember was that big ginger bastard, hoping that one day I'd get a chance to fuck him up.

I never did see him again.

Until now.

I awoke, my head pounding. I'd been laid out on a thin white mattress and stripped naked. As I groaned and rolled over, I saw another five guys laid out in a similar fashion. I sat up and looked around.

We were in a different room than before. Time had obviously passed and I had no idea how long we'd been unconscious. My feet had been bandaged and it looked like we'd all been cleaned up a bit. We must have been out for hours. The room had plaster walls and looked different from the warehouse and I guessed that we'd been transported to a different location. My throat felt dry and sore and my eyes stung but I otherwise didn't feel too bad.

At the end of the bed I saw a packet and opened it to find another pair of overalls. They were coloured in red and white stripes. My colours. I reached over and nudged Dobb in the leg. He stirred and looked at me with slitty eyes.

"What…. where the fuck are we?"

"I don't know. Get dressed and let's see if we can find a way out."

He groaned and slowly stood up, giving me a most unwelcome close up of his big hairy balls and cock. He pumped out a fart.

"For fuck sake!" I said, standing up and moving away a few yards to get dressed.

The other guys started to wake up. They looked around in confusion and rubbed at their eyes.

"What's going on?" asked one, looking at me as though I were somehow responsible.

I shrugged and started examining the walls of the room. There were two doors, both locked. A tv screen was mounted above one of them. I gave one of the doors a good kick and it didn't budge so I took a few steps back and tried again. Still nothing. We were trapped.

The other guys dressed themselves and I noticed they had different colours. One wore overalls with black and white stripes, another claret and blue. I walked over to him.

"Inner City Firm or Villa Youth?" I asked.

"Villa..." he said in a Birmingham accent, eyeing me with suspicion. "How do you know?"

"Your colours," I said. "All of us, we're dressed in our team colours."

"What does it mean?" he asked.

"It means that we weren't chosen at random."

As if on cue, the tv screen flickered into life. The Japanese woman was back.

"Contestants, listen!" she cried, still grinning like a maniac. "You best of best in British! In few moment, you meet best of rest of world. Fight to the death!" She erupted into a fit of giggles. She was replaced by an image of a rack of weapons. "Choose wisely!" she said. "Last man left win prize!"

The screen went dark but music continued to play. Happy, demented music completely at odds with the way we were all feeling. There was a clicking sound and one of the doors slowly opened. Dobb went through first and we all followed. Inside a new room the walls were lined with weapons. Axes, staffs, knives, swords, lances, you name it. There was another tv screen and high up in one corner a camera was watching us.

The Villa Youth guy started to cry.

"I want to go home," he said, his voice choked with emotion. "I can't do this."

"Pull yourself together, mate," said one of the others. "We're representing England now."

I looked at him with a mixture of horror and admiration. He'd simply accepted the situation for what it was. He walked over to the wall and took down an axe. When he looked back at the rest of us he was smiling. He looked insane.

Dobb reached up and took down a sword. He held it up in front of himself and then moved around a little with it to test how it felt. Satisfied, he lunged forward and stuck it straight through the guy with the axe. As the Villa Youth man screamed and covered his face, Dobb hacked up the other two guys as they panicked and reached for weapons. With three bodies on the floor he took a swing and cut deep into the neck of the Villa man, killing him instantly. When he looked up at me there was a glint in his eye.

I'd known Dobb for nearly twenty years but, at that moment, I had no idea whether or not I was going to be next. When he put the tip of the sword down onto the ground I finally exhaled with relief.

"All right?" he asked.

"What the fuck did you do that for?"

"You heard the lady – it's going to be every man for himself where we're going."

"But what about us, Dobb?"

"What about us?"

"What if there comes a time when it's just you and me left?"

"We'll worry about that if it happens. For now, it's going to be us against everyone else. We can work as a team."

"Don't you think these guys could have helped us?"

"I didn't know them. I didn't trust them. Any one of them could have fucked us over at any time. I just happened to get in early, that's all."

"Jesus, mate."

"You know I'm right."

At that moment, I didn't know anything any more. This was the single most insane, terrifying and ridiculous experience of my entire life and would undoubtedly, if I survived, define what I had left.

I'd spent most of my life around violence, either taking it or dishing it out. I thought I was used to it by now, thought I'd seen everything. In the past I'd been bottled, stabbed and even shot at. I'd been left for dead in a shop doorway in Hamburg and thrown over a wall in Tenerife. I'd done some terrible things to other people, hospitalising them, maiming them. But this was another level completely. This was actually killing people. I didn't know if I could handle this.

"You'd better tool up," he said, interrupting my thoughts.

"I'm not doing it, Dobb."

"What do you mean?"

"Like I said." I looked up at the camera and shouted at it. I had no idea if anyone was listening or if they gave a shit about what I said. "Fuck you! Who are you people? Tell me what's going on here or you can all go fuck yourselves! I want to speak to somebody in charge. You can't do this to us! Do you hear me? Is anybody listening?"

We stood there in silence. Dobb was looking at me with a mixture of pity and disgust. I could tell he wanted to speak but he kept his mouth shut. Just as it seemed as though nothing was happening, the door behind us opened and two guys in body armour and helmets stepped into the room. One carried a baseball bat with nails in the end and was adjusting the strap on his helmet as though getting to us had been a rush job. The other guy had a taser in one hand and a long dagger in the other.

The screen flickered into life and a man in a black suit stared into the room.

"Contestants," he said, his voice calm. "You need to continue. If you don't comply within thirty seconds it will be game over for you."

I looked at Dobb. He smiled at me and I knew exactly what he was thinking. He was ready to tear these fuckers apart. I turned to the rack of weapons and took down a set of throwing axes. When I turned back I nodded and Dobb and, without a word passing between us, we attacked the new arrivals.

They weren't ready for us. Unless you're a hooligan yourself, and you've experienced a tear up that can spark off in an instant, there's no way to prepare for the sudden violence that people like Dobb and I are capable of. I don't know where they'd recruited these guys from, maybe they were ex-police or ex-military, but handling yourself in an arrest situation, or even a warzone, wasn't preparation enough for an instantaneous flare up of intense violence in close quarters by ferocious animals like us. And we *were* animals, dirty bastard honey badgers with attitudes from Hell. Violence is like a switch for us, it can be turned on and off quicker than a lightbulb. We can be smiling at you one second and have a blade at your eyeball the next, ready to carve you up before you even get the chance to scream.

The ability for invoking total carnage at the drop of a hat isn't a skill you can put on your CV, but it's a skill all the same. I've seen people run from Dobb just because of the way he looks at them. A quick change of expression is enough. There's something in his eyes that can bore deep into the soul of another person and terrify them beyond measure. I know what it's like to give that look to someone and I know what it's like to receive it. The intensity, the sheer heat and aggression coming off it, it's like looking into a furnace.

I threw one of the axes and it lodged itself in the armour of the guy on the left. It wasn't enough to hurt him but it was enough to shock him for the time I needed to cross the room and hit him with the flat end of an axe head in the side of the knee. His leg collapsed, no doubt with ligament damage, and I kneed him in the ribs and followed him down to the floor. As Dobb put his sword through the other guys neck, I hacked away and broke apart my guy's helmet and started getting through to his face. He was screaming but that didn't last long.

When we were finished, Dobb and I stood up and walked back to the centre of the room.

"Your men are dead," I shouted at the face on the television set.

"So I can see," he said. I thought he'd be angry now but his voice was still calm. If anything, the corners of his mouth had turned up in a tight smile. No doubt the footage of what we'd just done would be used at some point and it was all good for him. "Why don't you tell me what you want," he said.

"I want to get out of this place," I told him.

"You can. Just finish the game."

"And if I don't want to?"

"Then i'll just keep sending more of my men into that room until they manage to kill you."

Dobb looked up at the camera and gave him the finger.

"Who the fuck *are* you?" I asked. "And where are we?"

"I'm Dan Whistler, Head of Operations," he said. "And it doesn't matter where you are."

"Why don't you just tell me anyway?"

"You're in the Ukraine. Does that knowledge make you any happier?"

"No, it doesn't."

"I didn't think it would. Can we get a move on? We're on a tight schedule."

"What is all this?" I asked him. "What are you doing to us?"

"You know what this is. It's a game show."

"So I keep hearing. This isn't like any game show I've ever seen."

"That's because it isn't *any* game show – this is something special and it's taken two years to plan. We're networked up globally and about twelve million people are about to tune in and watch you on the dark web."

"This is a joke, right? Some sort of 'gotcha' type shit?"

"It isn't a joke, Mr Penn."

"How the fuck do you even know my name?"

"We know everything about you. That's why you're here. Are we done?"

"No, we're not. This is illegal. People are dying!"

"Of course they're dying. Nobody would be watching if we gave you pillows to fight with."

"You can't hope to get away with this... Murdering people on live television."

"I'm not murdering anybody. You are. You both seem rather good at it, especially your friend there. We'll sell a few t-shirts with his face on, I'll bet."

I could tell I wasn't getting through to this man. I certainly wasn't going to talk him out of going through with this.

"Just tell me why we're here," I said. "Why us?"

"Because you and your friends are the worst kind of scum society has to offer and normal people have been sick of your antics for decades. All across the world, you gather in gangs and cause havoc, costing millions of pounds to deal with and clear up after you. Governments have tried to shut you down but nothing has worked. This is our solution."

"What, killing us?"

"No. Letting you kill yourselves. You people seem to want to get together and cave each others heads in and your confrontations have been getting increasingly violent. The only logical solution was to get you off the streets and to give you an environment and the weapons to do it properly. And, of course, to film it and put it on a pay-per-view broadcast. Everyone's happy, don't you see? The public aren't bothered by your violence, businesses aren't losing money shutting down while you terrorise the cities, you all get the chance to fight each other to your hearts' content and an audience bored of cinematic violence gets to see some of the real stuff. It's a win-win for everyone involved."

"Except for us," I said. "We're dying here."

"Everyone's got to die sometime," he said.

"The authorities will shut you down if word gets out. Twelve million people won't keep quiet about this. Footage of what you're doing to us will leak."

"Who do you think sanctioned all of this to begin with?" he asked, genuinely surprised that I hadn't realised.

"My own fucking government are involved?" I asked, incredulous.

"Of course. They detest you, Mr Penn. Now, are we done?"

I supposed we were. There wasn't a great deal I could do about any of this except go through with it.

"Just one last thing," I said. "The prize – what is it?"

"Your life," he said before the screen went black for the last time.

I stood there, shoulders slumped, thinking over his words. It was a lot to take in. This said, I could see his point of view. If I wasn't up to my neck in that shit I'd have been first in the queue to watch it.

"Ok, then," I said to Dobb.

"What are you going to choose?" he asked. "Those axes seemed to suit you."

I ran my eyes over the available options and saw something that leapt out at me. I had no idea why but it just felt right. I reached up and pulled a mace down from the rack. A spiked metal ball, attached to a chain and a heavy wooden handle, thumped into the floor.

"Good choice," said Dobb, nodding.

The door opposite clicked open and we walked down a long, brightly lit corridor. The sound of cheering, a chorus of thousands of voices, grew louder as we approached an opening and stepped onto a ramp leading down to a large arena. I took a few seconds to look around and take it all in. There must have been twenty thousand people in the audience. Down in the arena, dozens of other competitors were milling about in small groups.

"Are you ready to fuck some cunts up?" asked Dobb, smiling.

"All day long," I said.

Together, we walked down the ramp knowing that, at best, only one of us would be walking back up it when this was finally all over.

# Also Available by Steve Roach

## Short Story Collections
The Hunt and Other Stories
Resonance
Tiny Wonders

## Novellas
Ruiner
People of the Sun
Conquistadors

## Travel
Cycles, Tents and Two Young Gents
Mountains, Lochs and Lonely Spots
Step It Up!

## Non-Fiction
An Alternative Playlist
Arcade Retro Classics
Small People, Big World

## Illustrated Books For Children
Crackly Bones
The Terrorer

Printed in Great Britain
by Amazon